forever home

a dog and boy love story

HENRY COLE

scholastic press ♥ new york

author's note

not long ago, a dear friend of mine told me a story about a young boy named Greg. Greg wanted a dog . . . badly. He thought about dogs all the time. But Greg was a bit careless with his things. He had a hard time keeping his room in order and getting his chores done.

His parents worried that he wasn't disciplined enough to care for a dog. After all, a dog is a living, sentient being, requiring a very real commitment of time and energy and devotion. "You can't be a dog owner if you can't clean your own room," his parents told him.

Greg decided to prove just how disciplined and determined he could be. And like the boy in our story, he found an old leash and began walking it every day — morning, noon, and night. In sizzling sun or drenching downpour, Greg persisted.

As weeks and months passed, his parents saw his commitment was real. Ultimately, they took Greg to the pound to pick a pup! How truly great it was that Greg was able to prove his readiness and devotion to take on this great responsibility.

and how great it is to adopt a pet! So many animals are in need of good homes. It's been my experience that adopted animals can make the best pets: Often they've known the hardest of times and forever appreciate the love and security of a kind home.

Sometimes people move and leave their dogs behind, or sometimes people find that they cannot care for their dogs, so they set them free alone outside, where they have no access to food or safety or dry, warm shelter. There are millions of dogs that are abandoned and living a feral existence in the US alone. What a sad life for our best friend.

adopt if you can,
and share your life with a pet who longs for a
forever home.

FOR JETT — H.C.

LIBRARY OF CONGRESS CATALOGING-IN-PUBLICATION DATA AVAILABLE
ISBN 978-1-338-78404-6
10 9 8 7 6 5 4 3 2 1   22 23 24 25 26
Printed in Mexico   189 • First edition, July 2022

Special thanks to Jayne Vitale, Director, Education and Youth Programs, North Shore Animal League America for her expert advice and consultation on our book. And to Rachael Rudman, Senior Kennel Manager, North Shore Animal League America, for her sensitivity reading. • For information about Animal League America's Mutt-i-Grees Curriculum for social emotional learning, go to: muttigrees.org. • For other humane education programs go to: redrover.org/2019/12/04/a-humane-education-program-for-the-whole-family • teachheart.org.

Henry Cole's artwork was created with Micron ink pens on Canson paper. • The display type was set in ITC Esprit Bold. • The text type was set in Adobe Garamond Pro Regular. The book was printed and bound in Grupo Espinosa • Production was overseen by Catherine Weening. • Manufacturing was supervised by Shannon Rice. The book was art directed and designed by Marijka Kostiw, and edited by Dianne Hess.